Welcome
to the
Neighborhood!

by Becky Friedman

Simon Spotlight

New York London Toronto Sydney New Delhi

SIMON SPOTLIGHT
An imprint of Simon & Schuster Children's Publishing Division
1230 Avenue of the Americas, New York, New York 10020
© 2014 The Fred Rogers Company
All rights reserved, including the right of reproduction in whole or in part in any form.
SIMON SPOTLIGHT and colophon are registered trademarks of Simon & Schuster, Inc.
For information about special discounts for bulk purchases, please contact Simon & Schuster
Special Sales at 1-866-506-1949 or business@simonandschuster.com.
Manufactured in the United States of America 1214 LAK
10 9 8 7 6 5
ISBN 978-1-4424-9741-2
ISBN 978-1-4424-9742-9 (eBook)

It was a sunshiny day in the neighborhood, and Daniel and Prince Wednesday were playing at the castle. Suddenly, they heard the royal trumpet blaring.

"Hear ye! Hear ye!" cried King Friday, "A special visitor is coming to the Neighborhood of Make-Believe today!"

Daniel grinned at Prince Wednesday and asked, "Who could the special visitor be?"

Then Daniel had a grr-ific idea. "We should have a special Welcome-to-the-Neighborhood party for the special visitor!" said Daniel.

"That is a royally great idea, boys!" King Friday cheered.

"We can have the party at the Clock Factory," Prince Wednesday said. "We can have cake and decorations, and music so we can dance! Boop-she-boop-she-boo." Prince Wednesday wiggled his hips, showing off his dance moves.

Daniel jumped up and said, "Let's go to the music shop and ask Music Man Stan to play music at our party!"

Daniel and Prince Wednesday hopped on Trolley. "Trolley, please take Daniel and Prince Wednesday to the music shop." said King Friday. *"Ding! Ding!"* said Trolley.

"It's a beautiful day in the neighborhood," sang Daniel and Prince Wednesday as Trolley rolled toward Main Street.

"*Welcome to the Music Shop!*" sang Music Man Stan as Daniel and Prince Wednesday walked through the door.

"Hiya, toots!" said Miss Elaina.

Daniel and Prince Wednesday told Miss Elaina about the special visitor, and she got so excited that she began to jump up and down. "Maybe the special visitor is . . . a famous singer . . . like a rock star! I love singing. *La la la!*" said Miss Elaina.

Daniel imagined that the special visitor really was a rock star.

Daniel asked Music Man Stan to come to the party and play some music, and he agreed. "This party is going to be awesome!" Daniel said.
"It is. But right now I'm royally hungry," said Prince Wednesday.
"Let's all go to the bakery and get snacks for the party," said Daniel.
"It's a beautiful day in the neighborhood!" sang the kids as they headed to the bakery.

"Welcome to the bakery!" said Baker Aker.

"I'm watching the dough rise," whispered O the Owl. "Then Baker Aker will bake it into dinosaur-shaped bread . . . it's my favorite."

"Baker Aker, can you please bring some dinosaur bread to our special Welcome-to-the-Neighborhood party?" Prince Wednesday asked.

"It's for a special visitor," Daniel added.

"I'd be happy to bring dinosaur bread to the party," said Baker Aker.

"Who-hoo-hoo could it be?" hooted O the Owl. "Maybe the special visitor is a . . . a . . . a . . . dinosaur!"

Daniel imagined that the special visitor really was a dinosaur.

"Is it time for us to go to the Clock Factory now?" hooted O the Owl.

"Yes!" said Daniel. "We'll see you at the party, Baker Aker."

As the kids danced out the door of the bakery, they sang, *"It's a beautiful day in the neighborhood!"*

Daniel and his friends were almost at Clock Factory Park when they heard, "Meow, meow!" coming from the Neighborhood Café. It was Katerina Kittycat sitting with her mom, Henrietta.

"A special visitor is coming to the neighborhood," hooted O the Owl.

"It's going to be really super," added Miss Elaina.

"A special meow meow visitor?" said Katerina with a gasp. "Maybe it is someone super . . . like a superhero . . . or a mommy . . . or a *supermommy!*"

Daniel imagined that the special visitor really was a supermommy.

Daniel and his friends arrived at the Clock Factory. All of the neighbors were there too.

"Hear ye! Hear ye!" cried King Friday. "We have come here today to welcome a very special visitor to our neighborhood. And look, the special visitor is here! Do you know who it is?"

Suddenly Daniel smiled. "I see who the special visitor is!" Daniel said with a cheer. He ran to greet the special visitor. Daniel wanted to be the first one to say hello. Who is the special visitor?